Join the Cutiecorns
on every adventure!

Heart of Gold

The Purrfect Pranksters

Cutiecorns

Heart of Gold

by Shannon Penney
illustrated by Addy Rivera Sonda

SCHOLASTIC INC.

Puppypaw Island

PLAYGROUND

BEACH

FURMUSEMENT PARK

HANDYSNOUT'S HARDWARE

OUTDOOR THEATER

BARKING

FLASH'S HOUSE

FURBIDDEN FOREST

MISTYPAW MEADOW

GLITTER'S HOUSE

WOOFING

For Luke and Lucy, who make every day magical.

Text copyright © 2019 by Shannon Decker
Illustrations copyright © 2019 by Addy Rivera Sonda

All rights reserved. Published by Scholastic Inc., *Publishers since 1920.* SCHOLASTIC and associated logos are trademarks and/or registered trademarks of Scholastic Inc.

The publisher does not have any control over and does not assume any responsibility for author or third-party websites or their content.

This book is a work of fiction. Names, characters, places, and incidents are either the product of the author's imagination or are used fictitiously, and any resemblance to actual persons, living or dead, business establishments, events, or locales is entirely coincidental.

ISBN 978-1-338-54036-9
10 9 8 7 6 5 4 3 2 1   19 20 21 22 23

Printed in the U.S.A. 40
First printing 2019

Book design by Jennifer Rinaldi

Chapter 1

"I'm right on your tail!" barked Sparkle, chasing her friend Twinkle across a flower-studded field.

Twinkle slowed down for a second, turned around, and stuck out her tongue with a smile. "You'll never catch me!"

Just then, another pup streaked by them in a blur of fluffy white fur. "She might

not—but I will!" Glitter the Maltese puppy yipped gleefully.

Twinkle's jaw hung open in surprise. Sparkle couldn't help laughing. "Come on, Twinkle," she said, trotting up to her Beagle pal. "Get your paws in gear! Last one to the crab apple tree is an unlucky puppy!"

The two friends raced after Glitter. The beautiful horns on their heads glinted in the sunshine. After all, these weren't ordinary puppies—they were Cutiecorns!

The Cutiecorn puppies all lived together on Puppypaw Island, a special place brimming with magic and adventure. They looked just like regular puppies, but there was one big difference: They all had colorful unicorn horns! Their horns gave them each a unique magical power.

Sparkle and Twinkle ran side by side, closer and closer to catching Glitter. Sparkle put her head down, racing as fast as her powerful Golden Retriever paws would take her . . . until she heard a yelp up ahead. She looked up just in time to see a shadowy figure leap out from behind the crab apple tree!

Glitter, Sparkle, and Twinkle all skidded

to a stop, so scared they could hardly bark. Sparkle covered her eyes with one paw.

"Gotcha!" cried a familiar voice.

Sparkle opened her eyes to see the grinning face of a Yorkshire Terrier with a purple horn. "Flash!" she barked. "You scared us out of our fur!" Twinkle grumbled in agreement, and Glitter giggled.

"Sorry!" Flash said, dashing circles around her friends. "When I saw you racing, I just couldn't help surprising you at the finish line. You should have seen the looks on your snouts!" She leaped into the air. "Plus, I have some puptastic news!"

Sparkle's ears perked up. She could never stay mad at her mischievous friend for long. "What kind of news?"

Twinkle rolled her eyes, polishing her silvery blue horn with one paw. "This had better not be like that time she said she had a special surprise, and then made us watch for an hour while she moved a bone across the table."

"That was ter-ruff-ically impressive!" Glitter protested, grinning at Flash. "It was the first

time she'd moved anything using just her magic powers."

They had all played around with their powers a bit—Glitter tried to create a rainbow, and Twinkle once tried to turn her little brother into a toad—but they were just pups, so they hadn't learned anything official. They wouldn't really begin mastering their powers until they had their Enchanted Jubilee, a big ceremony to celebrate that they were ready to start using their magic.

Flash's excited smile grew even bigger. "This is way better than that time!"

"You always say that," Twinkle said.

"Hear me out," Flash went on, taking a seat near the trunk of the blooming crab apple tree. The other pups gathered under the canopy of purple flowers, too. "I was just walking through the market—well, I wasn't walking, it was more like running, because if my mom spotted me she would have made me help with—"

Sparkle cleared her throat.

"Right," Flash said. "Anyway, when I went by the fountain in the center of the square, I noticed Mrs. Horne talking to some of the other grown-ups. So I tried to be super sneaky. I walked really close to them so I could hear what they were barking about."

"You were eavesdropping?" Glitter asked, her eyes wide.

Flash thought for a minute. "Maybe," she said. "But I can't really help it if I was in the right place at the right time. And that's beside the point! I heard Mrs. Horne mention the Enchanted Jubilee."

Sparkle, Twinkle, and Glitter were suddenly all ears. Mrs. Horne was the respected Husky in charge of planning the jubilee for all of the young Cutiecorns. Was this the news they'd been waiting for?

"Did you hear any details?" Sparkle asked, feeling her belly flip-flop with excitement.

Flash jumped to her paws. She couldn't contain herself anymore. "She said the Enchanted Jubilee would be held on Friday! That's just three days away!"

Chapter 2

The pups all began barking at once.

"Three days!"

"Pawsome!"

"Hot dog, what great news!"

Flash's eyes shone. "Isn't it amazing? It seems like we've been waiting furever, but the jubilee is finally happening!"

The Enchanted Jubilee took place every

year at the top of Majestic Mountain. When each Cutiecorn was ready, they were invited to the ceremony, which was always planned behind closed doors. Sparkle, Glitter, Flash, and Twinkle already knew they were on the list for this year's jubilee. They had each passed the test earlier in the year. Now they finally knew the date of the ceremony! Thinking about it, Sparkle realized that she didn't really know what happened during the Enchanted Jubilee. It was tough to dig up details on such a big secret! All she knew was that afterward, she would begin training and learning to use her magic. Bow wow!

Glitter ran in circles around the crab apple tree. Her pink horn sparkled every time it

caught the sunlight. "I can't believe it! I just can't! Is this fur real? I have to get home to tell my mom!"

Sparkle nodded. "It's almost dinnertime anyway. Let's head home, pups!"

Barking and laughing, the four friends frolicked across the field. Everywhere they looked, colorful flowers peeked out of the green grass. The sun hovered above the tree-tops, casting everything in a warm glow. Flash picked a bright red poppy and tucked it behind Twinkle's ear. The Beagle stuck her snout in the air proudly. She had forgotten all about being grumpy!

When they reached the far side of the field, the pups continued along a dirt path that led back to town. Puppypaw Island was full of beautiful beaches, mountains, fields, and forests. Most of the Cutiecorns lived in and around Barking Bay, the town on the water's edge. There was a market, a playground, a big beach and splash pad, and even an outdoor movie theater! But the beauty of Barking Bay came from the Cutiecorns who lived there.

Their powers made sure every building was colorful and vibrant. Glimmering fountains dotted the streets. The roads were lined with archways of flowering trees. Breathtaking sights and smells were everywhere, and the air seemed to shimmer with magic! What more could a pup want?

The friends reached Glitter's house first, a little cottage surrounded by beautiful flower beds. (Glitter and her family were excellent gardeners because they loved to dig!) The little white pup nuzzled each of her friends affectionately. "Paws down, this is the most exciting news I've ever heard!" she yipped. "I don't know how I'm going to sleep tonight . . . or tomorrow night . . . or the night after that." She shook her head and laughed. "See you tomorrow, pups!"

The others waved and continued along the path. "Do you think everyone knows about the jubilee yet?" Twinkle asked. "Or is it still a secret?"

Sparkle thought for a moment. "We can't be sure until the official invitations go out," she said. She remembered last year, when the older group of Cutiecorns got their invitations to the jubilee. She'd been so jealous of her neighbor Glow!

"Well, they'd better arrive soon," said Flash. "You know I'm terrible at keeping secrets!"

Sparkle giggled. Flash had trouble keeping her barks to herself, that was for sure. But Sparkle couldn't imagine life on Puppypaw Island without her feisty, funny friend!

"I, for one, am glad you're a blabberwoof," Twinkle said, winking. Then she trotted up to her house, a sturdy wooden cabin with an elaborate obstacle course in the backyard. (The other pups loved playing at Twinkle's house!)

Sparkle and Flash headed down the block to Flash's beautifully decorated blue house. Flash's mom and dad were very stylish, so their house was stylish, too! It was surrounded by a huge yard—perfect for an energetic pup like Flash.

"Bye, Sparkle!" Flash yipped, doing a little backflip. "Next time I see you, we'll be one day closer to our jubilee!"

Sparkle felt her belly flip-flop with excitement again. She waved a paw and raced the rest of the way home, enjoying the wind in her fur. Moments later, she burst through the front door of her family's brick house. "Hey, Mom! Guess wha—oof!"

Before Sparkle could even finish her sentence, she was knocked off her paws by something fuzzy and yellow.

"It's here! It's here!" the little fluff ball barked over and over.

The little fluff ball was her younger brother, Zippy!

He nudged her with his nose, then darted into the other room. Before Sparkle could even lift a paw, he reappeared. This time, he was holding something in his mouth.

"Calm down!" Sparkle said, laughing. "What's that?"

"Mis ma mimmamamon!" Zippy mumbled around the thing sticking out of his mouth.

Sparkle grabbed it . . . and gasped. It was a shimmering purple envelope with her name on the front in fancy gold letters.

Could it be?

"It's the invitation!" Zippy barked.

Sparkle couldn't help cheering. Zippy howled with excitement for his big sister. The invitation to the Enchanted Jubilee was here. Now it was truly official!

Chapter 3

Sparkle opened her eyes the next morning and stretched, feeling warm and sleepy. Suddenly, she remembered the big news! She leaped to her paws and turned on some music. She felt like dancing!

As Sparkle pranced around her room, she heard the door squeak open.

"Good morning, twinklepaws!" Her dad

poked his muzzle around the corner. "Looks like you've got your tail in gear today." He winked.

Sparkle twirled around gracefully, like a ballerina. "The sun is out, I smell peanut butter pancakes cooking, and I'm going to start learning all about how to use my magic soon." She threw her paws in the air. "This day can't get any better!"

Her dad looked thoughtful. "Oh, no? Hmm. Well, you might want to dance on down to breakfast and see what tricks I have up my fur this morning." With a smile, he disappeared down the hall.

He didn't get far before Sparkle raced after him, tripping over her own paws. "Tricks? What kind of tricks?" she asked. Her dad was a master of shifting magic, and he liked to use it to play silly tricks on Sparkle and Zippy. They always had to be on their toes! "Tell me, tell me!"

Her dad laughed as they trotted into the kitchen. "See for yourself," he said, pointing a paw at the table.

Sparkle's place at the table had a heaping pile of peanut butter pancakes . . . but there was something next to the plate, too. It was a small golden box, topped with a bright, beautiful sunflower. Sparkle sat down, looking at it in awe.

Zippy popped his head out from behind a stack of pancakes on the other side of the table. "Open it!" he mumbled around a mouthful of food.

Sparkle's mom set a jar of maple syrup on the table and kissed Sparkle on top of her head. She was especially good at caring magic. Just being near her always made Sparkle feel safe and happy. "You might as well see what's inside the box, don't you think?"

Sparkle gently lifted the lid, careful not to crush any of the sunflower's delicate petals.

When she saw what was inside, she could hardly bark! On a bed of fluffy white cotton lay a shimmering golden locket in the shape of a heart. It had a swirly *S* on the front, and glittery designs etched around the edges. Sparkle knew this locket—it had hung around her mom's neck for as long as she could remember! Inside was a tiny photo of Sparkle and her family, all smiling from ear to ear.

Sparkle looked from her mom to her dad with wide eyes. She didn't know what to woof!

"Wow, cool!" cried Zippy, breaking the silence.

Their mom took the locket from the box and carefully fastened it around Sparkle's neck. "This was my locket, and Grandma Shimmer's before me. Her mom bought it

for her when she got her invitation to the Enchanted Jubilee. Learning magic is a huge responsibility, just like this locket. Take good care with both."

"I love it! It's the most beautiful thing I've ever seen! Thank you, thank you!" Sparkle said. She threw her paws around her mom, then her dad. "I'll take good care of it, I promise!"

"Oh, honey, it matches your golden horn perfectly," her dad said.

Sparkle darted over to the window and peeked at her reflection, turning from side to side and watching the locket catch the sunlight. "It's pawsome!" she barked. "I can't wait to show everyone!"

"Let's have some breakfast first," her mom said, pouring syrup on Sparkle's pancakes and grinning.

After a quick breakfast, Sparkle dashed off to Mistypaw Meadow to meet her friends. Who had time for extra pancakes when there was so much to do? As she ran, her new locket swung from her neck, making a little jingling sound.

"What's the hurry?" a familiar voice woofed.

Twinkle ran up next to her, ears flapping in the breeze.

Sparkle did a little leap of excitement. "I couldn't wait to show you all my new locket!" She turned her head so Twinkle could see it as they ran.

"Wow," Twinkle breathed. "It's pawfect! Isn't that your mom's?"

"Yes, but she passed it down to me because I'm responsible now!" Sparkle said proudly.

Just then, the road curved and Mistypaw Meadow stretched out in front of them. Flash and Glitter were up ahead, rolling on their backs in the grass.

"Hey, pups!" Twinkle called. "Check this out—Sparkle got a new locket to wear to the jubilee!"

Flash and Glitter gathered around, yapping in admiration. Sparkle sighed happily. She was surrounded by friends, the grass was tickling her paws, and the sun felt warm on her fur. Nothing could ruin this ter-ruff-ic day!

"Let's play freeze tag," Flash suggested. "Then we can go to my house for pupsicles."

The friends all barked in agreement.

"I'll be It!" Glitter called, and the other pups scattered to different parts of the meadow. Glitter raced after them, laughing as they darted out of her reach.

Sparkle ran to the far edge of the meadow, near a cluster of lilac bushes, with Glitter right on her tail. The little white pup reached out—and tapped Sparkle with her paw.

"Gotcha!" Glitter cried gleefully. Sparkle

groaned, giggling. Now she had to freeze in place until someone else freed her! She stood very still, watching her friends race around the grass.

As Sparkle looked on, something in the air shifted. She couldn't quite put her paw on it, but she felt strange and tingly. Her fur stood on end. She cocked her ears, frozen but alert.

Something was happening—but what?

Suddenly, she spotted a shadow out of the corner of her eye. Before she knew what was going on, something bolted by in a blur. Sparkle felt her collar lurch. She looked down in surprise. Her locket was . . . gone!

And now the thief was gone, too!

Chapter 4

Sparkle was so shocked she couldn't even bark. Her friends hadn't noticed anything unusual. They kept running around the meadow, laughing and woofing.

"I'm coming to unfreeze you, Sparkle!" cried Flash, ducking away from Glitter and zipping toward Sparkle. But when she saw the look on her friend's furry face, she skidded to a stop. "What's up, pup? You look like you've seen a ghost."

Sparkle shook her snout. "I didn't really see anything—that's part of the problem!"

Glitter and Twinkle trotted up, cocking their heads quizzically. Glitter gasped. "Where's your new locket?"

"Someone—or something—snatched it right off my neck!" Sparkle explained. "All I saw was a shadowy blur, and then it disappeared." She hung her head. What ruff luck! She couldn't even keep track of the locket for one morning. Her parents would never think she was ready to learn how to use her magic after this! She may as well forget about the Enchanted Jubilee now.

Flash clapped a paw over her mouth. Twinkle

frowned. Glitter gave Sparkle a hug. "Oh, that's just horrible!"

"It *is* horrible," Twinkle said suddenly, with a fierce look on her face. "And we're going to do something about it."

The other pups all looked at Twinkle in surprise.

"But what can we do?" Sparkle asked sadly. "We don't know who we're looking for or where they went. They could be miles away by now!"

Twinkle nodded. "You're right—but we have to try. You're our friend, Sparkle, and we're going to do everything we can to help you get your locket back. Let's put our snouts together, pups!"

Glitter and Flash cheered, and Flash did a

flip in the air. Sparkle couldn't help the little grin that spread across her snout. What pawsome friends she had!

The four pups settled down in a circle, right where Sparkle had been standing. "First, let's mark the scene of the crime," Twinkle said, jabbing a stick into the ground. "That way, we'll remember exactly where to search for clues."

"Ooh, we're just like real detectives!" Glitter yipped. "You're good at this, Twinkle."

Twinkle blushed but quickly tried to cover it up. "Okay, okay—focus, pups. The good thing about living on an island is that there are only so many places to hide."

"But what if the thief leaves the island?" Sparkle asked glumly.

"The ferry only runs on Mondays and Saturdays, remember?" Flash said. "Unless the thief is a fish, they're not going anywhere without that boat."

"That gives us plenty of time to investigate," Twinkle declared. "I think it would help if we drew a map of Puppypaw Island. We can mark places on the map that we want to search."

Twinkle pulled a piece of paper out of her backpack. As the best artist among them, Glitter got to work drawing an outline of Puppypaw Island. She added different land-marks as her friends suggested them—the beach, the playground, Mistypaw Meadow, Majestic Mountain, the Furbidden Forest, and so on. Before long, they had a ter-ruff-ic map!

"One last detail," Sparkle said, taking the pen from her friend's paw. She carefully drew an X in the very spot where they sat. It was the scene of the crime, after all!

"Now let's look around this area for any-thing unusual," Twinkle suggested. "Maybe the thief left something behind that will give us a clue."

All four pups got to their paws. They began

walking slowly and carefully around the far edge of the meadow with their snouts to the ground. It was silent except for wind rustling the tree leaves and birds chirping overhead.

Suddenly, Flash let out a flurry of excited barks. "I think I found something!"

Sparkle, Glitter, and Twinkle raced to her side as fast as their paws would take them.

Their friend was inspecting some strange marks on the ground.

"The grass is thinner here, see?" Flash pointed a paw. "You can see the dirt better. And don't those look like—"

"Tracks!" Sparkle barked excitedly. They had their first clue!

"You're right," Twinkle said. "Those don't look like Cutiecorn tracks to me. There are four toes on the paw, like a Cutiecorn pup, but the claw marks look longer . . . and sharper!"

Sparkle felt a shiver run up her back. "So if they're not Cutiecorn tracks, what are they?"

"Let's sniff around a little more," Glitter said. "Something definitely smells strange around here. Maybe we'll find another clue about who made those tracks."

"I'm not sure I want to know," Flash whispered to Sparkle. Sparkle giggled nervously.

After a few more minutes of silent searching, another bark rang through the air. This time, it was Glitter. "Look, look!" She pointed a paw at the trunk of a tree on the very edge of the meadow.

"Are those . . . claw marks on the trunk?"

Flash asked. "They look like the same sharp, jagged claw marks we found on the paw print!"

Twinkle nodded. "I think you're right. Whatever they are, they weren't made by any Cutiecorn that lives here!"

Chapter 5

Sparkle and her friends headed home that afternoon with a lot to bark about. It had been a ruff morning, but Sparkle felt confident that they were going to find her locket! Now, if she could just track it down before her parents noticed that it was missing . . .

After dinner, most of the Cutiecorns headed to the beach for a bonfire. It was one of

Sparkle's favorite summer traditions—Bonfire Wednesdays! Pups from all over Puppypaw Island gathered on the beach to roast marshmallows, watch the sun go down, and frolic in the warm golden sand.

As Sparkle set paw on the beach that night, she couldn't help smiling. The lights of Barking Bay shimmered off to one side, while the setting sun glimmered on the water. The sky was streaked with pink and orange. What a puptastic place to live!

"Sparkle! Over here!" Flash waved a paw. She, Glitter, and Twinkle were standing around the unlit bonfire with other Cutiecorns of all ages. Twinkle's dad was joking and laughing as he used his magic to bring the fire roaring to life. His horn glowed silver as flames rose into the air. Everyone cheered and clapped their paws, then grabbed long sticks for roasting marshmallows.

Sparkle trotted over to join her friends, with Zippy close behind her. "How many marshmallows do you think I can fit on one stick?" he asked, licking his lips. Sparkle giggled.

"At least six," Glitter said, pawing over a stick and a bag of marshmallows. Zippy's eyes grew wide. He ran off to the other side of the fire, yipping excitedly to his friends.

"I'm dog-tired," said Flash, plopping down in the sand.

Sparkle nodded. "Me too! We've had a busy day."

"And there's more investigating to do tomorrow," Twinkle said.

The four pals usually spent Bonfire Wednesdays playing volleyball or jumping waves, but none of them had the energy tonight.

"Let's just put our paws up and relax," Glitter suggested, digging out a seat in the sand.

They all settled in and sat quietly for a minute, watching the sun sink behind the water. Sparks from the fire shot into the air and crackled overhead.

Just then, a voice came from around the other side of the bonfire. "Haven't you heard? She has sleek black fur and yellow eyes . . ."

Sparkle's ears pricked up. Around her, Twinkle, Flash, and Glitter all sat up a little straighter.

"Did you hear that?" Sparkle whispered.

The others nodded. "I can't see who's barking, but it sounds like one of my brother's friends," Flash said. Her brother, Dash, was six years older and was puptastic at using his magic.

The voice on the other side of the bonfire continued. "Claw is a sinister wizard with amazing powers. Rumor has it that she's been prowling Puppypaw Island in cat form for many years, but she's rarely been seen. She spends most of her time in the Furbidden Forest."

Sparkle, Glitter, Flash, and Twinkle all looked at one another with wide eyes. An evil wizard in the shape of a cat? What a fur-raising thought!

Without making a sound, the four friends

got to their paws and slowly walked around the bonfire. The brown German Shepherd speaking was, in fact, one of Dash's friends. Lots of other pups, including Dash, had gathered around to listen.

"No one knows exactly what kind of powers Claw has, or why she came to Puppypaw Island to begin with," the German Shepherd

went on. "But we should all hope we never find out."

Sparkle shivered.

Twinkle put a paw around her shoulders. "It's just big pups telling silly ghost stories, you know that," she said gruffly. But she didn't look so sure.

Flash shrugged. "My brother and his friends do love spooky stories," she said. "But what if Claw is real?"

Sparkle couldn't help barking what she was thinking, even though she knew it sounded silly. "What if she's real . . . and what if she's the one who stole my locket?"

Glitter's eyes grew wide. "Oh, Sparkle, do you really think it could have been Claw?"

Sparkle's mind raced. Flying fur balls, everything was starting to make sense!

"I didn't see anything other than a shadow," she recalled, "so whoever stole my locket was fast."

"And we did find those strange paw prints with the sharp claws," Twinkle said thoughtfully.

"And claw marks on that tree!" Flash said with a gasp.

Sparkle nodded. "I was standing right on the edge of the forest, too. Barking Bulldogs, this could be our biggest clue yet!"

Twinkle looked thoughtful. "So let's say it was Claw who stole your locket. Why did she do it? And where did she go?"

"We don't know why she did it, but we know where she took it," Sparkle said with a shudder.

All four friends barked at once: "The Furbidden Forest."

Twinkle sat up straight, more determined than ever. "Then we know where we're headed tomorrow." She noticed the nervous looks on her friends' snouts. "Don't worry, pups. We'll stick together. And we're one giant pawstep closer to finding Sparkle's locket!"

Chapter 6

The next morning, Sparkle woke up bright and early. She felt jumpy, but she couldn't tell if she was nervous or excited—or both! Today she would work with her friends to try to recover her precious heart-shaped locket. She had to get it back! She'd been waiting her whole life to learn to use her magical powers. Now that she was so close, she couldn't let her parents think she wasn't ready for the responsibility. Bow wow, it was time to prove herself!

But they would have to go into the spooky Furbidden Forest. The thought of it made her fur stand on end!

Sparkle knew she had to get her paws in gear, otherwise thinking about Claw and their mission would make her even more nervous. She grabbed her backpack and headed downstairs.

Her mom was making eggs in the kitchen. "Good morning! Are you hungry?"

Sparkle's stomach did a little flip-flop. No, she definitely wasn't hungry. "Not yet," she said with a shrug, careful to turn away before her mom noticed that the locket was missing.

"Could I just take some snacks with me? I'm meeting up with Flash, Twinkle, and Glitter this morning."

Her mom looked at her closely, then smiled. "Big plans, huh? Sure, grab some fruit and granola bars." She gave Sparkle a hug. "Have fun! Remember, you can always ask for help if you need anything."

One of the best things about living on Puppypaw Island, Sparkle thought, was that the pups were free to come and go as they pleased. It was a safe place, and there were always adult Cutiecorns around to help.

As she headed out the door, Sparkle couldn't help noticing the shiver that ran down her back. Claw was dangerous. So was the Furbidden Forest. Sparkle felt a sharp pang of regret. She knew she should tell her mom about the locket, and about where she was heading. That was the responsible thing to do. Wasn't she supposed to be responsible?

Then and there, Sparkle vowed to be brave, but also to be smart. As much as she loved her locket, it wasn't worth putting herself and her friends in danger! If things got ruff today, they would leave right away. Sparkle let out a big breath, relieved at the thought.

Glitter, Twinkle, and Flash were waiting for her up the road. As usual, Flash was running in circles, ready and raring to go. Twinkle looked braver and more determined than Sparkle had ever seen her before. And Glitter was calm, with a sweet smile on her snout.

Glitter put a paw on Sparkle's shoulder. "How are you feeling?"

"Better, now that I see all of you," Sparkle barked. Her friends gave her courage!

Twinkle held up the map they had drawn the day before. Everyone gathered around. She pointed a paw at the edge of the Furbidden Forest next to Mistypaw Meadow, where they'd found claw marks on the tree. "This is our starting point. No matter what happens today, we stick together!"

All four pups put a paw in the center of their circle. "One . . . two . . . three . . . Cutiecorn crew!" they cried, lifting their paws in the air. They'd been doing that chant since they were little. Today, Sparkle was feeling more thankful for her crew of friends than ever before. Now, if

only they already knew how to use their powers, maybe this adventure wouldn't seem quite so fur-raising.

Flash dashed out ahead of the group. "Let's go!" she yipped. "Claw will never see us coming! With my lightning speed, Glitter's enthusiasm, Sparkle's brains, and Twinkle's grumpy attitude, we're unbeatable!"

"Hey!" Twinkle cried as the other pups dissolved into giggles. She chased after Flash, barking and laughing.

The pups saw Mistypaw Meadow stretching out in front of them in no time. The green grass seemed to glow in the morning sunlight. On the other side of the meadow, thick trees reached toward the sky. Compared to the bright, colorful meadow, the Furbidden Forest looked like a wall of darkness. Sparkle felt that familiar shiver ripple through her fur.

Twinkle fearlessly led the way to the edge of the woods. Checking her map, she paused next to a towering tree. "Here are the claw marks. Sparkle, which way did you say the shadow moved when it took your locket?"

"It came from over here, near this tree," Sparkle said, "and went in that direction." She pointed a paw.

"Then that's where we start," Twinkle said firmly. She had a brave look on her snout, but Sparkle could tell her friend was just as nervous as the rest of them.

Sparkle, Twinkle, Flash, and Glitter squeezed paws, took deep breaths, and stepped into the Furbidden Forest. They walked slowly, carefully—even Flash. Leaves rustled overhead, and dry pine needles crunched under their paws. It was definitely darker in the forest, but once her eyes adjusted, Sparkle found that she could see just fine. Maybe this wouldn't be so bad after all.

The four friends walked along in silence for

a while, unsure of what they were looking for. More claw marks? Strange paw prints? A few times, they saw marks that looked like they could have been made by Claw. They followed whatever small clues they could find deeper and deeper into the forest.

The tall trees surrounding them all looked the same. Which way was Mistypaw

Meadow? Sparkle wanted to be brave—after all, her friends were doing this for her!—but her heart was starting to beat faster and faster. They hadn't found Claw . . . and now they were lost!

"Um, guys?" Glitter whispered just then. "Where are we, exactly?"

Twinkle frowned at her map. "I thought Mistypaw Meadow was back that way, but we turned so many times that I'm all spun around." She sighed.

Sparkle was starting to feel very strange. Was she panicking? This didn't feel like the time she'd panicked when she first jumped off the dock into the bay, or when her brother had tumbled down the steep hill by the beach and she had to race to stop him. No, she definitely felt different this time. Tingly, somehow. She couldn't quite put a paw on it.

"Sparkle!" Flash barked, so suddenly that it almost made Sparkle jump out of her fur. "Your horn! It's glowing!"

Suddenly, Sparkle knew exactly what she was feeling. Her magic was warning her of something . . .

Danger!

Chapter 7

"What's wrong, Sparkle?" Glitter whispered. The whites of her eyes stood out in the dark forest.

"There's danger close by," Sparkle said, looking around wildly. She couldn't see anything. She couldn't hear anything. But somehow, she knew. She felt tingly all over now. Her fur stood on end. Was this her magic talking to her?

"I don't see anything," Flash said, scanning the trees.

Twinkle's nose twitched. "Everything in this forest smells strange, so I don't think my nose is going to help us."

Glitter hadn't taken her eyes off Sparkle. "Use your magic," she said quietly. "You can do it, Sparkle."

Sparkle closed her eyes and tried to concentrate on feeling her magic. *Which way should we go?* she thought. *I don't need my locket back. We just need to get out of here! But how?*

Before Sparkle's magic could give her any clues, she heard a gasp from Flash. Her eyes flew open.

Slinking out from behind a grizzled old tree was a sleek black cat. Her fur blended into the dark forest so well that she looked more like a rippling shadow than an actual cat. She had glowing yellow eyes, sharp claws, a spiked collar . . . and Sparkle's golden locket around her neck!

"Claw," Twinkle breathed.

All four pups huddled closer together. Sparkle could feel her friends shaking in their fur. They were really up to their snouts in trouble now.

"Ah, visitors," Claw hissed, stepping toward them. "Little Cutiecorns! How adorable. What are pups like you doing in the Furbidden Forest?"

Claw sat down a few paces away and stared at them with gleaming yellow eyes. Her black pupils widened menacingly as she watched the pups. Sparkle had never seen eyes quite like these—they seemed to freeze her in place!

Luckily, Flash still had her wits about her. "We've been looking for you, Claw!" she said bravely, holding her snout high.

Claw's eyes flickered, and a smile spread slowly across her face. "Me? I'm honored."

Twinkle found her voice. "Yes, you. That locket around your neck belongs to our friend Sparkle here. You stole it."

"It's special to her," Glitter added fiercely. "We've come to ask for it back."

Since Claw had appeared, Sparkle hadn't been able to bark a single word. She had felt frozen in her fur! But seeing her friends stand up for her so bravely gave Sparkle courage.

She took a step forward. "Please, we don't want any trouble. I'd just like my locket back. Then we'll leave you alone."

Claw laughed, a strange, hissy sort of laughter. All four pups flinched. "Oh, you will? Lucky me." Her eyes narrowed. "Unfortunately, I'm not planning to paw over this locket. You may not know this about us felines, but we love anything sparkly. I've had my eye on this locket for years." She licked one paw slowly and used it to smooth back her whiskers. "I didn't dare try to steal it from your mom, little pup, but snatching it from you was the purrfect solution."

Sparkle's mind raced. Of course it wasn't going to be that easy. They had been silly to think that Claw would give back the locket . . . and even sillier not to come up with a plan for what to do next. Now they had to think fast in order to save their fur!

Flash was watching Sparkle very closely. Suddenly, she began talking a mile a minute, asking Claw questions and telling long, rambling tales.

"So, what brings you to the Furbidden

Forest? It's so nice to finally meet you—we've been hearing stories! You're just like I pictured, though your eyes are a lot glowier than I'd expected. They're really amazing! Do you have good night vision? It seems like that would be handy in a place like this."

Twinkle and Glitter looked at each other and shrugged, but Sparkle knew just what her friend was doing. Sparkle needed time to think, and Flash was giving her that time!

Claw couldn't get a word in edgewise. She surely wouldn't listen to Flash ramble on forever, though. Sparkle had to be quick on her paws.

Flash was still talking. "So, do you have other cat friends? Where are you from?"

Sparkle knew the pups couldn't outrun

Claw. She was agile and fast, as she'd proved
when she stole the locket. Sparkle remembered how she'd streaked by in a shadowy
blur, so fast that Sparkle couldn't even see her!
The pups couldn't overpower Claw, either. She
was sleek but muscular, and her claws were
shiny and sharp. Sparkle didn't want to get
anywhere near those things.

"You seem really fast," Flash rambled on as Sparkle thought. "Have you ever run in any races? I love to run . . ."

No, they wouldn't be able to outrun Claw. They wouldn't be able to overpower her. Just then, Sparkle felt her golden horn tingle, and a ter-ruff-ic idea appeared in her head. Maybe, with some help from their magic, they could outsmart her!

Chapter 8

Sparkle suddenly had a plan—a good one. She felt sure that it would work. She'd never felt so sure about anything before! Could this have something to do with her magic?

There wasn't time to wonder about it. They had to get their paws in gear!

Flash was still barking on and on, and Claw seemed to be losing her patience with the chatty pup. "Those claws of yours are really fabulous!" Flash said. "So pointy! Do you have them professionally sharpened?"

Sparkle quickly whispered her plan in Twinkle's and Glitter's ears. Then she stepped up next to Flash and put a paw on her shoulder. "Let's leave this poor cat alone," she said. She gently led Flash back behind the others, filling her in under her breath.

In the meantime, Twinkle stepped closer to Claw. Sparkle could see her silvery-blue horn twinkling faintly. "We're sorry to have bothered you," she said, watching the cat carefully. "We'll just be going now. Enjoy the locket."

Claw was speechless for a moment. She stood very still, staring at the pups with her piercing yellow eyes. As they turned to leave, she took a few steps after them. "Not so fast."

Still facing away from Claw, Sparkle smiled. Twinkle was incredibly good at understanding others. She had said just the right thing! Claw didn't know it, but she was playing into their plan. She'd stepped to the exact spot where they needed her to be.

"Oh, did you need something?" Glitter asked sweetly.

Claw sunk back on her haunches, her body and head low to the ground. She was getting ready to pounce!

"Now!" Sparkle barked.

Everything seemed to happen all at once. Flash and Glitter stepped in front of their friends, horns suddenly gleaming in the darkness. Glitter stood very still, her eyes fixed on Claw. Positioned to pounce, Claw seemed frozen to the spot. Glitter's magic was keeping her there!

Flash's purple horn glowed more strongly now. She narrowed her eyes, concentrating hard. As she did, the locket around Claw's neck began to move. It lifted slowly at first,

then faster, until the chain had gone right over
Claw's head. The locket flew through the air
and into Flash's paw! Flying fur balls, it took
everything in Sparkle not to cheer out loud!

Claw let out an angry yowl. But under
Glitter's gaze, she still couldn't move!

Without missing a beat, Flash tossed
the locket over her shoulder to Sparkle. But

the little Cutiecorn wasn't done yet! Two sticks zoomed through the air toward Claw. They crisscrossed through her spiky collar. The ends of the sticks jabbed into the ground, rooting Claw in place. That should slow her down for a while!

"I hope we'll get to chat again soon!" Flash called to Claw.

"Okay, pups, let's get out of here," Sparkle barked. Her locket swung around her neck as she turned to leave.

Together, the four friends raced through the woods as fast as their paws would take them.

Sparkle's horn lit up the dark woods with its golden glow. She could feel the magic coursing through her. This time, she knew just how to get back to Mistypaw Meadow. Her magic was guiding her!

Flash giggled as they ran. "I've never seen a cat look like such a sourpuss! Claw had no idea what hit her!"

"That was some puptastic shifting magic you did back there, Flash," Glitter barked. "The locket and sticks moved exactly where you wanted them to go!"

"I'm not even sure how I did it!" Flash said. "But I couldn't have done it if Twinkle hadn't lured Claw to the perfect spot, and if you hadn't used your magic to keep her there."

Twinkle nudged both pups along with her nose. "We're not in the clear yet," she said gruffly. "Let's save the congratulations until we know our tails are safe!"

The friends dashed on in silence. Their paws pounded on the dirt and fallen leaves. Four sets of paws ran as fast as they could go.

Was it four sets of paws? Sparkle slowed to a trot, listening hard.

Flash, Glitter, and Twinkle nearly bumped right into Sparkle. "What is it?" Glitter asked quietly.

"Do you hear that?" Sparkle said, her eyes wide.

Sure enough, even though the pups had slowed down, the sound of running pawsteps still echoed in the forest.

Someone was running after them!

"Claw must have escaped from our trap faster than we expected," Twinkle said, breaking into a run again. "Go, go, go!"

Breathing hard, the four Cutiecorns bolted through the forest faster than they had ever run before.

Sparkle felt panic rising in her chest, but she forced it back down. She had to concentrate on feeling her magic, and letting it guide them out of the woods.

"There's a break in the trees up ahead!" she woofed over her shoulder.

"It's Mistypaw Meadow!" Flash cried.

Sparkle could see glimpses of the sunny meadow through the thick, gnarled trees. Just a little farther! If they could get back through the meadow and to the busy part of town, they'd be safe.

Claw wouldn't dare follow them out into the open . . . would she?

Chapter 9

Sparkle burst through the last of the trees and into Mistypaw Meadow, with her friends close behind. They all skidded to a stop beyond the trees, panting.

"I've never been so happy to see Mistypaw Meadow before," Glitter said, trying to catch her breath.

"You can bark that again," said Twinkle.

Sparkle held up a paw, listening hard.

The sound of pawsteps behind them hadn't slowed down. They were coming closer!

The four pups looked at one another with wide eyes. There was nowhere to hide in the wide-open meadow. They didn't dare go back into the woods. There was only one thing left to do.

"Run!" Flash cried, taking off across the meadow. "Again!"

Racing after her, Sparkle kept sneaking peeks back over her shoulder. Whatever was chasing them would be out in plain sight any minute now. Sparkle could see tree branches near the edge of the woods moving as something thundered past . . .

"Hey, wait up!" a voice called.

A bundle of golden fur tumbled out of the shadowy woods, rolling head over paws into the grass.

Sparkle stopped so quickly that Twinkle and Glitter crashed into her. Scrambling to her paws, she shook her snout, trying to clear her head. "Zippy?!"

The bundle of fur stood up. "Yeah, it's me,"

said Sparkle's little brother. He walked toward them, looking sheepish.

Glitter, Twinkle, and Flash all stared at the pup with open mouths. "Boy, am I glad you're not an angry cat," Flash said.

"What are you doing here?" Sparkle barked.

Zippy wouldn't look right at his big sister. "I may have overheard you guys talking about your plans—by accident. I felt terrible that your locket had been stolen. I just wanted to help you get it back! So . . . I followed you."

Sparkle leaned down until she was snout-to-snout with Zippy. "That was so dangerous! The Furbidden Forest is no place for a pup!"

"To be fair," Glitter said gently, "it's no place for us, either. We're lucky we escaped."

Sparkle nodded. Her friend was right. She had led her friends and her little brother into danger. She looked down at her locket, sparkling in the sunshine.

"I'm so sorry," she said. "I never should have let you all risk your fur for me. No locket is that important!"

"We wanted to help," Twinkle said. "You didn't make us do anything, Sparkle."

"And it was wrong for Claw to steal your locket right out from under your snout," Flash yipped. "We showed her not to mess with the Cutiecorns!"

Zippy grinned. "Yeah, you did! I saw the whole thing." He looked down, embarrassed. "I may have been hiding behind a tree. Those yellow eyes were so creepy that I froze in my fur! Some help I was."

"I'm just glad you're okay," Sparkle said, nudging her brother.

The five pups walked across the meadow and down the path toward town. They were all quiet, lost in their own thoughts. Sparkle's locket swung back and forth as she walked. It had been special before, but now every time she looked at it, it reminded her just how much her friends and family loved her.

Zippy cleared his throat, breaking the silence. "That was some really cool magic you did back there," he said with a smile.

Flash jumped in the air, unable to contain herself. "Right?! It was so pawsome! None of

us have ever used our magic like that before! I
guess danger really brings it out of us! Imagine
what we'll be able to do once we actually have
lessons in how to use our powers. We're going
to be unstoppable!"

Twinkle rolled her eyes. "Let's not put the tail
before the snout," she said with a groan. Then
she grinned. "It *was* pretty ter-ruff-ic, though."

"I felt all tingly, like the magic was moving

through every strand of fur on my body," Glitter said.

Sparkle ruffled Zippy's fur. "You'll learn to use your magic soon enough, too, little brother!"

As the five pups came to the top of a hill, Barking Bay stretched out below them. The colorful little buildings looked so safe and familiar. Beyond them, the ocean glimmered in the afternoon sun. Just seeing it, Sparkle breathed a huge sigh of relief.

"I think I could sleep for a hundred years after all that excitement," Flash said.

Glitter laughed. "Don't sleep too long, Flash—you wouldn't want to miss our Enchanted Jubilee tomorrow!"

Sparkle felt a thrill of delight run through her. Tomorrow!

Chapter 10

"Quit dragging your paws, pups!" Flash called, running up ahead of her friends.

"Not even escaping from a wicked cat wizard can tire her out," Twinkle grumbled, rolling her eyes.

Sparkle giggled, looking ahead along the path. It was a steep slope, but they were almost at the top of Majestic Mountain. Beyond Flash, she could see colorful streamers and balloons bobbing in the breeze—the jubilee site!

A long line of excited Cutiecorns followed behind them, chatting and laughing as they made their way to the Enchanted Jubilee. There were other pups their age who would be participating today, plus their families and friends. It seemed like almost all of Puppypaw Island was climbing the mountain!

Sparkle's whole family came up behind her. "It's time! It's really time! Hot dog!" Zippy barked, running in circles and jumping into the air. "Aren't you excited, Sparkle?" her little brother went on, trying to catch his breath.

"Ter-ruff-ically excited!" Sparkle declared, putting a paw to her locket. She had told her parents the whole story the night before. At first, they had been upset that she and her friends had done something so dangerous. But they were also impressed with her courage, her use of magic, and the fact that she took her responsibility for the locket so seriously. Sparkle knew that being responsible was important, but now she knew that it was always okay to ask for help.

Sparkle's mom had also revealed that the stories they'd heard about Claw had gotten way out of paw. She wasn't a sinister wizard at all, just a lonely cat who slunk around the forest looking for shiny objects to add to her collection. Whew!

Her dad nudged her with his shoulder. "We're proud of you."

"You're really ready to start using your magic," Sparkle's mom added.

As they reached the top of Majestic Mountain, Sparkle could hardly believe her eyes. The sun shone down on hundreds of beautiful flowers blanketing the grass. Streamers and balloons waved from poles all around the mountaintop. In the center was a stone platform that glittered silver in the sunlight. The sky was a crisp, bright blue. It was all absolutely pawfect!

"Wow," Glitter breathed, stepping up next to her.

Flash ran circles around them. "Can you even believe it? Isn't it pawsome?"

"It really is," Twinkle said.

The rest of the Cutiecorns filed in and settled in front of the stone platform.

"This way, pups!" called Mrs. Horne, gesturing to the young Cutiecorns. They gathered around her, yipping excitedly. Besides Sparkle, Twinkle, Flash, and Glitter, there were eight other pups their age who would be participating.

Mrs. Horne smiled at them all kindly, looking at each pup with her crystal-clear blue eyes. "This is a big day! I know you're all ready. Should we get started?"

All twelve pups cheered.

"Okay, follow along!" Mrs. Horne said. "I'll walk you through the whole thing. Just keep your eyes on me!"

The pups stepped onto the platform one at a time. They stood in a long line, facing the crowd of familiar, smiling faces. Everyone in the crowd began to clap and cheer.

Sparkle put a paw to her golden locket. This was it!

"Good morning!" Mrs. Horne said, waving a paw for silence. "Welcome to our annual Enchanted Jubilee. The pups you see before you will start to develop their unique Cutiecorn powers. Under the instruction of myself and my fellow teachers, they'll spend the coming years identifying their magic and learning to use it." She winked at the pups. "And they'll have a lot of fun, too."

Mrs. Horne then led the group of pups through the special Cutiecorn oath. "Repeat after me: I pledge to work hard and use my magic for the good of all Cutiecorns. Pup's honor!"

Sparkle and her friends repeated the oath solemnly.

Mrs. Horne grinned. "And now for my favorite part—the bracelets." As she held out a handful of glimmering bracelets, her turquoise horn began to glow. "These charm bracelets all have one charm on them right now, a Cutiecorn horn. As you learn more about your magic, you'll earn additional charms. When I call your name, please take a step forward."

Everyone knew that Mrs. Horne had truly incredible magic powers, but she was a master of seeing magic. This made her puptastic at understanding others, and especially at identifying their magical skills.

She went down the line, calling each pup by name and presenting him or her with a breathtaking golden charm bracelet.

When it was Sparkle's turn, she stepped forward and held out her paw. Mrs. Horne fastened the charm bracelet around it. As her horn shone, she announced, "Sparkle, your feeling magic is very strong. I can't wait to help you learn to use it."

A huge barking roar rose from the crowd. "Go, Sparkle!" her family cheered. Zippy jumped up and down with excitement, clapping his paws and barking at the top of his lungs.

Sparkle looked out at her family, then down at her glistening bracelet. She would remember this moment forever!

She watched as each of her friends were given their bracelets. Mrs. Horne pointed out Glitter's strength in caring magic, Flash's in shifting magic, and Twinkle's in seeing magic—just like Mrs. Horne herself! Twinkle blushed furiously, but she couldn't keep the happy smile off her snout.

As the final pup received a bracelet, the crowd cheered again. Mrs. Horne led everyone off the platform, holding up her paw for a high five as each pup stepped down.

"Ter-ruff-ic job, Cutiecorns!" she said. "I'm looking forward to working with all of you. I'll see you for lessons starting next week!"

The pups erupted into a flurry of excited barking and yapping. Flash ran over and

crushed Sparkle, Twinkle, and Glitter in a hug. "We did it!" she cried.

The four friends held out their paws, admiring their matching bracelets.

"Aren't they puptastic?" Glitter said, sighing happily.

Sparkle nodded. "And you know what's even more puptastic? All of the magical adventures we have ahead of us!"

About the Author

Shannon Penney doesn't have any magical powers, but she has ter-ruff-ic fun writing about them! If she were a Cutiecorn, she'd have a turquoise horn and the ability to turn everything to ice cream. For now, she'll settle for the ice and snow of New Hampshire, where she writes, edits, and goes on adventures with her husband, two kids, and two non-magical cats.

DON'T MISS THE CUTIECORNS' NEXT ADVENTURE: THE PURRFECT PRANKSTERS

Chapter 1

"Do it again, Flash!" Glitter giggled, clapping her paws.

Flash concentrated really hard. She focused all her energy on a dandelion growing along the side of the road. Her purple horn gleamed. The dandelion suddenly rose into the air, almost as if it were plucked from the ground by an invisible paw. It zoomed over to Glitter and tucked itself behind her fluffy white ear.

"That was puptastic!" Glitter barked. "Bow wow, you're getting really good at using your shifting magic already, Flash."

Flash grinned proudly, holding her snout high. "Thanks! It's so much fun finally learning to use our powers, isn't it?"

The two pups lived on Puppypaw Island, a pawsome place filled with rolling meadows, windy dirt lanes, and golden beaches. Barking Bay, the town at the center of it all, was bright, bustling, and brimming with magic. That's because the pups who lived there weren't ordinary dogs at all. They were Cutiecorns! Each pup had a colorful unicorn horn on his or her head—and magical powers to go along with it.

"Thanks for waiting," came a voice from

behind them. Twinkle, their blue-horned Beagle friend, joined Flash and Glitter at the end of the lane.

"Twinkle!" Flash yipped, running circles around her pal. "Want me to use my magic to pick a dandelion for you?"

Twinkle rolled her eyes, smiling. "I would love that, but I think we need to get going. We shouldn't be late for school!"

The three friends trotted along toward school, barking up a storm as they went. They paused at a little brick house along the way to pick up Sparkle, a Golden Retriever with a shimmering horn to match her fur.

"What do you think we're going to learn today?" she asked, falling into step next to Flash.

"I don't know!" Flash said, giving a little

leap of excitement. "But whatever it is, I'm sure it will be ter-ruff-ic!"

So far, Cutiecorn Academy was even more pawfect than Flash had dreamed it would be. The teachers and other pups were furbulous, and Flash had never imagined all the different kinds of magic they'd get to learn. It was a pup's paradise!

As the pups crested Howl Hill, they could suddenly see all of Barking Bay spread out below. Off to one side, the water stretched out all the way to the horizon. Small boats were docked in the cove at the bottom of Howl Hill, and Flash could see her dad's familiar blue boat tied to the dock. Cutiecorn Academy sat nestled in the hillside, gleaming white among the green grass and blooming flowers.

"Race you!" Flash yapped, taking off before her friends could even bark. She heard them laugh as their paws thundered along behind her. She may have been small, but Flash was fast!

Suddenly, she felt herself tumble snout over paws. She turned somersaults, finally rolling to a stop.

"Flash, are you okay?" Glitter appeared at her side, a look of concern on her snout. Sparkle and Twinkle were right behind her.

Flash grinned. "I'm fine—I must have just stumbled over my own four paws!"

Sparkle stepped forward. "No, you didn't." She held up the end of a long daisy chain, woven together with little white flowers, grass, and . . .

"Is that . . . seaweed?" Flash asked, poking the chain with her paw.

"It sure is," Sparkle said with a nod. "Strange! This chain was stretched across the hillside path."

Twinkle took a closer look. "It seems like someone was trying to trip up pups."

"What about the seaweed? Whoever made this chain must have come from down by the water," Glitter noted thoughtfully.

Flash got to her paws and wrapped the daisy chain into a neat loop. "Well, they got me, but let's make sure no other pups become falling fur balls." She set the chain off to one side of the path. "Before my ter-ruff-ic tumble, I believe we were racing!"

Without another word, Flash took off as fast as her paws would carry her. She raced under the school archway with Glitter, Sparkle, and Twinkle right on her tail. They all tumbled into a heap on the grass in front of the building, panting and howling with laughter. No sooner had they caught their breath, then a chime rang out. They had arrived just in time—school was starting! The four friends got to their paws and headed through the open doors to their classroom.